fractured

Fractured Lit Volume 3
Stories Selected by Peter Orner
Edited by Tommy Dean

Front cover and interior design
by Cynthia Young and Julianne Johnson

ISBN: 979-8-9882557-8-9

fractured

volume 3

contents

introduction

I'm on a bus on 93 South heading to Boston from New Hampshire. It's late. There's traffic. On the monitor above the seat in front of me Tom Hanks is playing Mister Rogers. He's unbuttoning his sweater. I'm not watching. Nobody's watching. It's a silent, parallel universe hovering above us in the darkness. A few moments ago, I fell asleep and woke up with my head on the shoulder of my seatmate. He was nice about it. He asked if I wanted to trade seats so I could rest my head against the window. I could have kissed him. November of 2023 and there are still such gestures of gratuitous humanity. I don't know your name. I'll never know your name. You and me on the Concord Coach outside Peabody. They pronounce it Peabuddy. Something just happened. Maybe I make too much of it. But it's always been my deeply clung-to belief, and this is about the only dogma I can get behind, that many of the great stories of our lives are the tiniest. A gesture, a glimpse, a moment. A common characteristic of all the stories that make up the book you are holding is that they are all short. This isn't the most important thing. What I've taken away from an inspiring few weeks of reading and rereading is that these are all artfully compressed universes. Compressed is not a synonym for short. It's always a question of what we leave out, no matter how many pages we are talking about. (Proust is compressed. He left out even more than he put in.) There's so much richness here, so many gestures, glimpses, moments. In these varied universes, so much happens: big things, small things, many of which I'm going to remember. A woman name Judith doesn't hide because nobody else is hiding, even though hiding might well be a good idea.

There's a story right there. Another woman puts on an apron as someone outside honks for her to hurry up. An entire scene in the contradiction of putting the apron on and the impatient honk, no? Another character is in the kitchen making a sandwich when Alan Henshaw, of all people, comes running through the backyard. What's he doing? Chasing something? A cat? Yet another character reaches out a hand to a wolf. Holy shit. Still another mother—we will never run out of stories about mothers—keeps the door open during a tornado because she wants to hear the sound it makes. Someone else scrubs a week's worth of onions off some dinner plates. Why does this detail move me so much? And some sentences need to be quoted verbatim: "It reminded me of a jock in high school who I overheard saying that toothless women give the best blowies." This brought me back to 1987, to something a coworker said when I was a bagboy at the Dominick's supermarket out on Route 41. I won't repeat it here. But isn't this what evocative stories do? In this case, one line sent me back 36 years to a crude (yet memorable) offhand comment I had, till then, forgotten all about. Another line that's just got to be set down here, this one an opening: "It was supposed to be chess club, but instead it was Gambler's Anonymous, and that's what you get in Moline." I've spent a few days in Moline (nice town), but you need not have ever been in an Illinois river town to take in the truth of this line. We've all got our Molines. And consider the contents of a dead father's briefcase, the case he was never seen without, the one that was almost an extension of his very arm. What's in the briefcase? Or take two actors pantomiming a shoe salesman and customer. Can't you see it? You see people pantomiming, even in this case when they aren't great actors, and somehow you see this ordinary, everyday occurrence in a whole new light. A strange thing when you think about it, to watch someone try on a pair of shoes. Chekhov said he could write about anything, including an ashtray, and then he went and did it. I'm not sure the master could have contemplated writing one out of submissions guidelines. And here, too, are fathers who touch their daughters' toes to say good night, and there are daughters who turn into birds. All this and so much more. Someone writes a letter to Dante's Beatrice on a receipt for leather shoes. There again. You see what I'm saying? In this anthology there is a person who writes a letter to a literary character on a receipt for leather shoes. Don't forget to mark your calendar for World Naked Gardening Day, which if it doesn't exist beyond these pages, it should. Have you ever heard a baby humpback whale breathe for the first time? Or how about a guy who simply must kiss the inside of his lover's knee? My favorite part of this is that the lover doesn't understand this fetish but nonetheless is patient. Another gratuitous kindness, perhaps. Perhaps not. And then there was a rain bomb. That was the year the houses washed downriver like a parade. And know this: steelhead trout do not know who their half-siblings are. Whether fish can identify their relatives—something I've never considered. Have you? I offer my reverence to the writers who have created these stories out of their wonderfully odd and warped imaginations. My thanks to you all, and to Tommy Dean and the good people at *Fractured Lit*, it's been an honor.

—*Peter Orner*

1

At My Job I Work the Robotic Arms

KATI FARGO AHERN

On the line, I run a double forklift. It's a lot like a regular forklift, but the forks both spread out on either side and when they fan out, you have to catch the grooves of both pallets just so at the same time. And you have to do it FAST. Also, the balance point is trickier, especially if your pallet is stacked high with empty plastic disks that won't get blown out from forms into bottles till later down the line. The disks weigh nothing, and it is a lot harder than it sounds. Also, on line 5, I work the robotic arms until they stop working, and I call the engineer.

When we are at work, Eugene talks about fantasy sports and the gun he has tucked away in his car. Anthony talks about superhero comics. Greg got so high he ran a forklift off the loading dock and needed a drug test and a lawyer. Anthony died last week at age 43.

At home, my daughter screams in the middle of the night if she has to cough or needs to pee. She plays with He-Man figures and My Little Ponies that we saved in a box for her. My wife gets drunk on boxed wine that saves for 30 days, but she has a hard time making it stretch for three.

At night, when my wife takes a shower, she meticulously swipes the edge of her razor blade against the bar soap because sometimes she gets mad and cuts herself. One time, the bleeding on her wrist didn't stop for four days. But she doesn't want to get flesh-eating bacteria from a warm, wet razor blade, so she cleans the blade against the soap. It creates deep, angry, soft grooves. The news says flesh-eating bacteria may be in all 50 states. Sometimes, she just showers, opens the door, and watches the paint peel on the ceiling because the fan doesn't work. Other times she shampoos and washes and then flicks four quick strokes against her skin so they look like bloody-beaded, five-lined music. Beyond a doubt, but full of hesitation.

WHEN I AM at work, I need to take a fifteen-minute break that my partner will cover. But my partner is so slow that I need to get him set up for my break so we don't get behind. I sit in my car and watch videos on my phone and eat a sandwich light on the lunchmeat, heavy on the mayonnaise. When it's hot, I need to turn the car on to run the AC. I dip my barbeque chips into the edge of my sandwich mayonnaise. I close my eyes and see the afterimage of line 5.

I have a friend who calls me when he's driving across town to pick his family up Chinese takeout. We get 15 minutes or so of catch-up on the kids, our wives, or some shows. Sometimes he tells me about some basketball or the latest fight. My wife says, "How's Scott? How's Joan?" and I don't like to say because when our breaths are counted, we haven't said that much.

MY DAUGHTER HAS a hard time at school. She writes her name in a kind of cursive she made up with a snake coming off the "t" like a sort of balloon. The snake is smiling. She calls it "snakeish." Her teachers tell us to let her do it. When she writes thank you notes or cards to my dad or my wife's mom, we include a parenthetical. We neatly print her message or her name. We explain what she means.

When the robotic arms stop working, there are a few things I do before I call over the engineer. I can punch a few buttons in a sequence, and sometimes, he doesn't have to come. When he comes over, he comes over like he thinks he's a god. His steel-toe boots are specially made because one of his legs is noticeably shorter. He walks with a limp. He smirks like a turtle. His teeth are braces-straight where each tooth looks a little too blunted, a little too uniform. His breath smells like mustard.

North Carolina is a "right to work state," which is the same as saying you have no rights to work at all. It's steamy-hot in the summer, and the winter is a surprising mess of gray sleet and icy rain. There's good music and good shopping. The people drive on I-40 like they'd never like to get home. Like they are driving 90 mph for their lives or just finding out. My wife and I would like to move away someday, but we can't decide on where we'd go. Our dog is so old he wears diapers inside. Our daughter watches the same movie on repeat.

One of my wife's friends holds a book club every month at her house. She makes themed food, and 16 ladies act like they have read the book. When I come home, my wife is always holding a book but never reading it. She either grips things too tight or touches so gently it's like bathwater. You'd wonder how she ever picks anything up. One time, her friend asked about me.

"Does Jake like to go out after work and share a beer with his friends on the line?"

My wife said she just blinked.

"I don't think he has any friends on the line."

If I'd been there when her friend asked, I'd have also said no. When I get home, I go to sleep. I touch my daughter's toes to say good night. I count her breaths and wonder. The next day is almost ready to begin.

KATI FARGO AHERN is an associate professor of English in the Professional Writing and Rhetoric Program at SUNY Cortland. She received her MFA in 2007 from George Mason University. When she is not writing fiction, her other academic research on sound, writing, and soundscape design can be found in journals such as *Computers and Composition* and *enculturation*.

2

Unfinished Equations

RENEÉ BIBBY

I stand at the kitchen window, calculating the parabolic arc a murmuration of birds makes against the ridge of conifers. He coalesces at my elbow, tipping his moon face up to me, to the scratch of blue sky beyond the box of this house. No longer a boy-shaped smudge or a specter.

You're supposed to find children charming—I'd learned that lesson early. Oh, other mothers would say, looking fondly at their boys, don't you hate to send them off to school? I'm a blade that cuts—sharp—and kids are tender things, better that my boys were in classrooms or sports practices or running wild through the neighborhood with a pack of others.

It's an unkindness now, some cosmic karma that in this new house I'd bought precisely because it suited just me, that I should have to put up with someone else's kid. His little pit-pats sound as he moves around the place at all hours, energetic as a Tasmanian devil, flicking on lights and devices, chattering, and peeping around corners as if I were more entertaining to watch than any nature program.

A hundred mental orreries of our orbits, but none of my calculations can predict when or for how long our worlds would pull far enough apart for there to be only pure and creamy quiet, only to spin into conjunction again so that we are shadows to each other. There is no calculus to solve the gravity that crashes us together, clear, solid souls in the same space.

I could say something now about the mechanics of how birds fly, and he'd hear me. He'd drink it, gulp it down like ice water on a hot day. His eyes are their own creatures. They are alive in his face. They tremble. They are braced for a boo! The whole of him is braced.

His mother had called from the kitchen, "What's that goddamn song you're humming?"

I'd glimpsed his mother, too. Late at night alone at the kitchen table, hunchbacked and hair loosening from a ponytail, or tying on aprons early morning as someone outside honks for her to hurry up. She is spilled gasoline. She is the slick-black of his life, the lung-searing choke, and the shimmer of fumes that begs for the tiniest spark to ignite.

I **DO NOT** understand the physics that binds me here. What purpose do I serve if I cannot snatch his words from the air to stop her from hearing his reply, "It's the song the lady in my room sings."

SHE IS AT his doorway, a scribbled face of rage: "Don't you fucking talk about her. She's not real!"

She's looked right at me in the hall, she's locked eyes with me entering the bedroom that used to be mine, she's heard my humming, too.

"You're humming, again," he says, at my elbow. "What is that song?"

The impulse to maintain the charade of distance rises up in me, a tsunami. But we are not separate. I cannot save him from his mother—worse, I was the reason for her conflagration. So, I say, "I am contemplating elliptic curves, L-series, infinite numbers, and fixed points. I am thinking of the art of solving the unsolved and dedicating your life to that which only exists in theory. Is the unfinished work what keeps me here?"

He's not like either of my boys, who would not have stood still for my philosophizing. He's careful to be neutral and quiet, but the animals of his eyes have softened, delighted to finally hear me.

His joy at something so simple is unbearable to witness. I look away.

"What difference it would make if I solved anything unsolvable. Who would even know? Nobody but a little boy. I am watching birds and trees through glass because I can no longer be amongst them. And I am humming Toccata and Fugue in D minor. Because it is beautiful. But I don't think you should hum it anymore where your mother can hear."

He absorbs all of that with a tiny nod and turns closer to the window, strains to stand at the same eyeline as me, seeking the birds who have already fled, as I am the shadow bound to this house. Or to the boy? A tender, trembling thing, who makes me wish for a body and warmth and presence again so that he might feel my hand brush the top of his head, down his shoulder to soothe every part of him that is burned and trembling and alive.

RENEÉ BIBBY (she/her) is the director of The Writers Studio Tucson, where she teaches beginner and advanced creative writing workshops. Her work has appeared in *PRISM International, Luna Station Quarterly, Third Point Press, The Worcester Review*, and *Wildness*. Her stories have been nominated for Pushcart Prizes and Best Small Fictions. Reneé is involved in the writing community as the coordinator of Rejection Competition and Tucson-based Write Wednesday weekly writing meetup.
Tweets @specialfeather
reneebibby.com

3

Odds and Ends

BRETT BIEBEL

It was supposed to be chess club, but instead, it was Gambler's Anonymous, and that's what you get in Moline. That's what you get in church basements. It might be fried chicken, or it might be stale donuts, and I should have left right then, but I didn't. I stayed. I don't know why I stayed. I wrote "Reg" on my nametag, which was maybe the first lie, and some guy was talking about basketball. He said that CBS music made him feel whole and complete and ready to bust through a wall, and he was going to listen to it tomorrow. He was going to watch every minute of every game he could. Every TV in his house was plugged in in the living room. He'd already called in sick. His heart rate was going to rise, and he would cry and scream ecstatically by himself, and it was going to be okay because he was a goddamn force of titanium will, and he swore. Swore to Christ. There weren't going to be any bets.

It's hard to describe exactly how the room reacted to this. You're not supposed to judge, I guess. You could tell, though, people thought it was a real shit idea, and I sat there, trying to hide my face. Trying to hide it without putting anything in its way, and I smoked a cigarette with this guy, after the meeting. He called himself Bigby. He said, "You don't look right," and the air smelled all cold and refreshing and dead, and I thought about all kinds of possible responses. *Who does, though*, or *Fuck off, asshole,* or maybe just kind of walk off like that. Like a goddamn scene from *Chinatown* or whatever, and all this must've taken forever because Bigby dropped some ash on my boot. I looked up.

"Seriously, man, you look like shit."

"Drowned rats," I said.

"What?"

"I used to walk in the door after practice, and my mom would say that. 'You look like a drowned rat.' I never really think about stuff like that."

"I don't think about much of anything."

"Because thinking is overrated, I bet."

"Don't bet."

"All bets are off," I said, and I also think I fucking winked.

Bigby shook his head a couple of times, and then he left like I should've, and I followed him, followed him all the way home. Safe distance. Lying back and letting these pickups tuck in between. His house was in that part of town by the interstate, and there was a lot of brick and lawns trying as hard as they could, and he had a big front window. You could see practically the whole first floor. There was a picture of Jesus and an Old Style sign, and the real obvious thing was there was not one fucking TV. A bookshelf. Christmas tree lingering. I thought about how maybe the screens were all in the basement or all under lock and key or some shit, and I don't know, man. Something about March. Something about snowmelt. It asks some pretty fucked-up questions, and I drove home thinking about all of them. Lies upon lies, and all I remember is the lights of the Burger King. Maybe that french fry smell is the only thing true.

BRETT BIEBEL is the author of *48 Blitz* (Split/Lip Press, 2020), a collection of flash fiction set in Nebraska. He has two forthcoming collections, *Winter Dance Party* (Alternating Current, 2023) and *Gridlock* (Cornerstone, 2024). His reader's companion to Thomas Pynchon's *Mason & Dixon* will be released by the University of Georgia Press in 2024.

4

The Cloud Lab

MEGAN CALLAHAN

In science class, Margot teaches them about the magic of snow. "Evaporation, condensation, deposition," she says. On the whiteboard she draws shapes connected by wiggly arrows. She's tall and wiry, spine curved from decades of bending over small desks. Her face crumples like paper when she smiles or laughs. The kids like her white hair, her billowy floral dresses.

Margot peels open a cardboard box and distributes the musty contents: boots and wool socks; fleece-lined ski masks; colourful snowsuits with drawstrings at the waist. She leads them down the hall in a bumbling single file. Her own coat seems to swallow her; she hasn't worn it in decades. "Gloves on," she beckons. "Let's go, zippity-zip." At the end of the corridor is a plain white door. *Cloud Lab*, the sign says. *Caution: Extreme cold.*

The lab has milky walls and a high, vaulted ceiling. A digital thermometer reads -40°C. The children squeal and marvel at their misty dragon breaths. They race across the room, cheeks red as hibiscus petals. At the control panel, Margot twists a dial and punches in a code. A humidifier hums beyond the walls, pumping in air saturated with water vapour. Soon the domed ceiling is foggy with clouds.

"When I was little, we had blizzards." Margot stamps her boots for warmth. "Clumps of snowflakes you could catch on your tongue." Her students stare and blink. The word flake confuses them.

"Like cereal?" a girl asks.

"No," she laughs. "No."

She talks of snow piling on rooftops. Burying cars. Three feet, five feet. "Up to your waist! We could swim in it," she insists. They groan and roll their eyes. She reverse-twists the dial and the humidifier quiets. "We'd pack snow in our fists and build forts in the yard. Barrel down hills on flimsy plastic sleds." Above them, the clouds grow like swirling cotton candy. "And the cold," she exclaims, throwing up her hands. "It prickled like needles. Chilled you to the bone."

One boy laughs, another pelts questions: Was it dangerous, the snow? Could you be smothered or drowned? They've never felt anything like the Cloud Lab before. Cold is for ice cream; AC in peak summer; lakes when you cannonball from sun-drenched docks. None of them know winter. None of them know bone-chilled. Margot bites her lip. She gropes for clear answers. Every year, she runs the experiment and tries to explain. Something is missing, something has been lost, but she can never find the words to describe why it matters.

And suddenly it's snowing: a sprinkling, like confetti. The children fall silent. They squish shoulders and look up, captivated by the magic trick. Arms above their heads, mouths open, tongues out. Margot folds her hands and presses them over her heart. She remembers frost on windows, darkness in the street. And the rhythmic crunch-crunch of her father, shovelling.

"Touch it," she encourages. "Each snowflake is different." Her students catch flakes and slip-slide in their boots. They scoop up mounds and try to eat them before they melt. "More!" one girl chants, but Margot shakes her head no. The school has water restrictions: a strict weekly limit. But already they've lost interest. They complain about cold toes. Margot ushers them into the hall, where they immediately shed their layers. Snow puddles from their soles onto the speckled linoleum. Margot gathers their snowsuits. She unbuttons her coat. Somewhere deep inside is an ache that feels like homesickness, except she's lived here her whole life.

Back in the classroom, the windows are open. The air is sweet and heavy with the scent of lemon trees. Along the road, the cacti bloom. Aeoniums reach for the sun.

MEGAN CALLAHAN is a fiction writer and translator born and based in Tiohtià:ke/Montréal. Her short stories have appeared in magazines like *Carve*, *FreeFall*, *Nashville Review*, *Room*, *PRISM International*, and in *Best Canadian Stories 2021*. When she isn't writing, she enjoys painting botanicals and spending time on her balcony garden.

5

Maid in America

CHRISTINE H. CHEN

When I go in, the sink is bursting with unwashed dishes coated with moldy leftover scraps, half-filled glasses, cups that balance precariously on the counter rim, ripped-open TV dinner boxes thrown on top; there isn't room for me to set aside the cleaned dishes. The washing skills I've practiced back home come to good use.

"It's real simple," Lisa said, on my first day. "Just Windex the windows, Lysol the kitchen floor, Clorox the towels, you know, and then, Mr. Clean the toilet bowls, there's also upstairs…"

THIS IS NOT the country of brooms and pans, coconut brushes, or Pledge oil my mother used to shine our armoires. This is new territory. I'm learning that Americans can make verbs out of proper names. There are specific products with different colors for a given task.

Upstairs is a big room filled with a jumble of chairs and stools, various artwork framed in all shapes and sizes, boxes of clocks, oversized clothing, a jagged landscape of abandoned animals. I wipe bodies of deserted things with a cloth, rinse it with warm water, repeat. In the end, they still look the same. Forlorn and unclean.

Downstairs, Lisa pulls out a blue ice pop from the freezer while I have my arms soaked in a bubble bath of Palmolive detergent. I'm scrubbing a week-old worth of stuck grilled onions on dinner plates.

"Want one?" she says.

I shake my head with a smile, resist the temptation to ask why it's blue, if it tastes like Windex in her throat, what she'd call that shade of blue.

"Where're you from again?" she asks.

At this point in my life, I'm reluctant to speak English because I know I have a weird accent. When I tell her where I am from, her eyes grow big. I can see her mind goes in loops. "Oh, is that in Malaysia or Australia?"

I hate to disappoint her. She's a nice lady in her thirties, long blonde hair, freckles on her cheek that remind me of a cheetah. There's a boyfriend with Oreo crumbs stuck on his T-shirt that lurks around sometimes. She doesn't make me vacuum her bedroom. I've never seen her bedroom. She pays me $20 every Friday, enough to buy a nice stack of letter paper decorated with music notes and red violets to write to my parents back in Madagascar, a T-shirt with the Golden Gate Bridge, and I still have extra dollar bills saved in a Danish cookie tin.

I explain that it's a big island in the Indian Ocean. She says, "Oh right!" like she got it. I know. I'm confusing. I'm a dark Asian girl who speaks with a melange of accents Americans can't put their finger on.

She sits back on her couch, licking her frozen blue ice, her eyes fixated on the screen where there's a couple who's yelling profanities at each other. *Fuck you, go fuck yourself, piece of shit, cunt.* I love saying American curse words when I'm alone in my dorm room. They don't mean anything to me, but they are sharp, decisive bursts of sounds I imagine screaming from the open top of a Chevy on a deserted road, hair whipping in the air, like in the movies.

CHRISTINE H. CHEN was born in Hong Kong and grew up in Madagascar before settling in Boston, where she worked as a research chemist. Her fiction has been published in *Tiny Molecules, Gone Lawn, The Pinch, CRAFT Literary, Hobart, SmokeLong Quarterly, Gordon Square Review, Lunch Ticket, Pidgeonholes, trampset,* and other literary journals. She is a grateful recipient of the 2022 Mass Cultural Council Artist Fellowship and the co-translator from French of *My Lemon Tree,* forthcoming in 2023 by Spuyten Duyvil. Her publications can be found at www.christinehchen.com.

6

Brain, Brian

WHITNEY COLLINS

Marvin's tumor is the size of an unshelled walnut. His doctor, who wears bile-colored Crocs, has told Marvin and Marvin's wife, Cathy, that he plans on removing the tumor with a knife that's not really a knife but a beam of light. When the surgery was first explained, Marvin saw a hot spatula cutting cold cheesecake, but now that the operation is tomorrow, he keeps seeing a red, plastic flashlight pointed at a dense, winter wood. *Who goes there?* He hears the surgeon call out, gleefully. *Make yourself known!*

THE NEUROSURGEON IS as young as Marvin's son, Brian. Brian no longer speaks to Marvin. Brian lives in Arizona with a girl Marvin and Cathy have never met but whose name is Begonia. They've seen a picture of their son and this girl. A dog that looked like a coyote was also in the picture. "Who wants a cartoon for a dog?" Marvin asked Cathy. "Who wants a houseplant for a girlfriend?"

MARVIN WAS A terrible father, but the tumor has lessened the reality of this. The larger the tumor grows, the better the father Marvin was. And the faster Marvin walks, the faster the tumor grows. Which is why, every morning, he goes to the mall in his big white shoes, the ones that look like loaves of junk bread, and walks 8,000 steps. He walks the length of Pinesap Plaza 14 times, back and forth, and as he does, he recalls things he thought about doing with Brian as things he actually did. Camping under a swirl of stars. Shooting clay pigeons. Making cowboy beans in a cast-iron frying pan. "There's Orion," he hears himself say. "More pintos?"

IN THE EARLY-MORNING mall, the managers raise the gated storefronts with much audible ado. The mall fountains sputter to life. Together, the fountains and the gates sound like static, and Marvin's mind becomes the roaring space between canyon walls. He passes stores. There's Queen B., Banana Pants, Mr. Stupid. He stares at the things for sale and cannot remember what they are for. He imagines a pair of underwear on a potted begonia. A woman's yellow sweater on a coyote. A whoopee cushion as a map of Arizona. Marvin moves his big white shoes faster. He forgets Brian's thin shoulders and crystalline singing voice. He forgets Brian's pitiful deer eyes, his milkweed hair.

Instead, Marvin remembers throwing a football that was never thrown, laughing at a joke that was never cracked.

At the end of Marvin's morning walk is Sprinkles, the ice cream kiosk. If Marvin times it right, he takes his last step when Dashel, the ice cream boy, flips over the OPEN sign. "Good morning, Marvin," Dashel says. "The usual?" Marvin's excitement is such that he can only nod. His head nods and the tumor nods, and fireworks go off in Marvin's mind—red and green and violet.

Dashel scoops the vanilla while Marvin watches. It's a sphere of snow rolled through a pristine field, the belly of a snowman that Marvin and Brian did and didn't build. Dashel rolls the vanilla through rainbow sprinkles, a brain dragged through artificial memories. He puts the ice cream into a paper bowl and places a shelled walnut on top. He hands the ice cream to Marvin, and Marvin goes and sits on a bench by the fountains. Every morning, he sits there until the ice cream has melted and the sprinkles have bled, and all that remains is the walnut, floating in gray matter. Tomorrow, Marvin will have his brain, but today he has Brian.

WHITNEY COLLINS is the author of *Big Bad*, which won the Mary McCarthy Prize, a Gold Medal IPPY, and a Bronze Medal INDIES. Whitney is also the recipient of a Distinguished Story nod from *The Best American Short Stories*, a Pushcart Prize, a Pushcart Special Mention, the 2020 American Short(er) Fiction Prize, and winner of the 2021 ProForma Contest. Her stories have appeared/will appear in *American Short Fiction*, *AGNI*, *The Idaho Review*, *Gulf Coast*, *The Pinch*, *Grist*, *The Best Small Fictions 2022*, and *Tiny Nightmares: Very Short Tales of Horror*, among others. Her second collection, *Ricky & Other Love Stories*, is forthcoming June 2024.

7

Patrons

HILLARY ANN COLTON

The shades are pulled down by Mick before the summer sunsets. Mick is a regular: he spends every day, open to close, in the bar drinking Bacardi and Cokes and shots of Fireball. He buys drinks for everyone and tells them he loves them. He loves me the most; he's proposed seven times.

His facial veins match his red hair, and his arms are speckled in bruises that are as dark as frostbite. He's in his early sixties with an adopted teen at home. He tells people his wife died from a flu vaccination, but he told me once that her body couldn't take anymore, and he doesn't talk about her until closing time.

Mick throws a fifty down and says he's gonna pick up a pizza on the way home. "Coming back?" I say.

"You know it," he says.

And I do.

BUFFY REFUSES TO sit on the left side of the bar because she has Mac D. She's been divorced five times and loves to talk about her sex life. Most people sitting at the bar top have seen at least one of her nipples. Buffy drinks vodka sodas in a pounder and needs a napkin to wipe the lime off her hands after squeezing.

She tries to hook her straw with her fat tongue and asks about me. I've learned my lesson with this question: no one actually wants to know.

"Great," I say, smiling and hopping a little. I feel happy after taking a shot in the back.

"I have a date for WNGD." Buffy grabs her phone and shows me a picture. She's already told me this, so I know that WNGD stands for World Naked Gardening Day. She is 62, and not only does she have a better sex life than I do, she is confident enough to pull weeds naked while a man she met online watches.

A woman I've only just begun to recognize scoots down to sit by Buffy. She tells us about her tomato plants: where to get them and how to nurture growth. We don't care, but we pretend to.

WHEN MY PATRONS ask me how I am, I say I'm good—busy, but good. I could say that my life is messy, and I move from toxic to toxic, and I spend my time watching Kim K tutorials on how to contour my face in hopes that I'll make more money if I am no longer myself. *I'm good; I'm busy* gets me a nod and smile as if my Daddy were calling me a good girl after I fetch him another beer.

MICK'S BACK, AND he says all his kid wants to do is play video games. I could say that it's his fault because he's never there, he's here, but instead, I get us shots. "Damn kids these days," he says.

I POUR BEERS for the men and vodka for the women and shake sugary liquor for the newly-legal. I allow myself a shot for every hour that passes because I tell myself I can't handle the drunks when sober.

Mick sits by Buffy and makes jokes about her wet, wet pussy, and she laughs like she genuinely means it. People play pool together and request that I turn the volume up on the jukebox when their song comes on. Unfamiliar faces come and go and play pool and throw darts and dance and laugh and touch.

A KEG BLOWS, and the tap sprays my face with white foam, making my mascara look wet. "I bet that's not the first time someone's blown in your face!" Clint says, a patron who wears four-hundred-dollar cowboy boots and blazers and sells things on the radio. When I swivel the new keg to its place, my boobs nearly fall out and catcalls follow. I laugh like *Oh well!* and give them a little shake as I readjust.

MY OLDEST PATRON is named Dick, and he used to direct plays on Broadway. Without fail, he tips two bucks. He offers me fifty to take him out back and show him the girls. "Maybe for your birthday, Dicky." I wink. He'll be 82 in January, and I hope he'll die by then so I won't have to.

The barback shows up, and we take a shot together. He hugs me, and the women tell us how cute we are, and the men pretend not to be jealous. We take a shot, and I know he's in love with me, but I have a boyfriend that no one knows about because he isn't allowed in the bar. Boyfriends are unpredictable, and mine's a Gemini, moody like fire. According to the Zodiac Gods we are destined for each other. I don't feel it when he's cold, like winter mornings, but when he's warm, I am a fucking queen. I am everything.

A MONTH LATER, the tomato lady disappears, and it's because she died of liver failure. Everyone at the bar will take a shot and cheer. "To the nice tomato lady!"

In the new year, Lo, the pizza guy who drank Coors Light, will overdose. I just saw him the other night. "He was sitting right there," we all say.

Jenn will crash her Honda into a nail salon. She was trying to quit, but the tremors—she lost control.

Mick's doctor will tell him to quit drinking, and for two days, he'll switch to beer. A young drunk woman is scared of a man who got her a cab, so I sit her down and say, "Don't move." When I look up again, she'll be gone.

Steve will get a DUI, and we'll all forget about him.

An employee and friend will die of a seizure after two months of sobriety. We really loved her. We'll attend her funeral and drink to her favorite shot: Tuaca and Red Bull. We'll look at pictures of her when she was in her twenties, and we won't recognize her because she wasn't pickled.

WE CRY AT our losses and devour our poison and tell ourselves that only the good die young, so full of life, and we swear we won't be like them.

We won't.

HILLARY ANN COLTON is an Idaho native and an MFA candidate in Boise State University's MFA program. She is currently working on her first novel and lives in the Treasure Valley with her family.

8

Launch Day Conditions: 1986

ELIZABETH CONWAY

Kerry found a hundred-dollar bill at the gas station near pump three. It was covered in oil. She carried the money inside to show the attendant, Jeremiah.

"A hundred bucks! What are the chances?" Kerry said.

"Lucky," he said.

She bought two cans of Dr. Pepper, and Jeremiah counted out her change. She slid him back a five.

"Lucky," she echoed.

When she got home, Kerry called her sister. It was Sunday. Kerry always calls her sister on Sundays. 6:45p.m. sharp. She told her about the hundred. The sisters agreed Kerry should buy a bus ticket and come down for a visit. Greyhound was offering a $55 roundtrip to Florida at the end of January; she would even have some mad money left over to burn. Lucky.

KERRY BELIEVES IN luck. Believes in routines. She performs even the most mundane—like brushing her teeth two minutes on the top with her right hand and two minutes on the bottom using her left—in predictable patterns. Kerry doesn't believe everything she does brings good fortune, but she's unsure exactly which routines, which actions, control her fate, so she stays committed to them all. Like the Sunday phone calls and now the Dr. Peppers. She buys them again and again, carrying them home in the pockets of her brown jacket. The cuffs frayed; its last three buttons lost long ago. Kerry dares not throw it out: a good luck uniform.

KERRY PACKS HER clothes in layers: shirt, shorts, shirt, shorts, then adds a heavy windbreaker—Florida can be unpredictable. On top of her clothes, she puts a framed photograph of herself and her sister at the Minnesota State Fair. In the picture, her sister is a toddler, and Kerry—six years older—holds her sister propped securely on her hip. They are standing next to a brown calf. Like the sisters, the cow looks directly into the camera. That was the year the tornado hit Fridley. It took out their barn, 22 of their cattle, 13 people. Kerry and her sister hid in the laundry room, under the sink. The sky was yellow and green. Their mother kept the front door open. "I want to hear what it sounds like," she said. She could hear a train. There wasn't a train. The state fair calf survived. They sold it to a farmer from North Dakota, and for the rest of the summer, Kerry slept in the laundry room. Her mother didn't argue. The summer storms waned. Later—later—when the summer passed, when the storms moved on, Kerry moved back into her bedroom, and her sister's appendix burst. In the room they shared, Kerry listened to her sister cry in pain and pulled her pillow over her head to muffle the moans that kept her awake. In the morning, their mom wiped vomit from her sister's mouth before placing her in the truck to drive to the hospital. She stayed for a week. At home, Kerry stripped her sister's bed and washed—and rewashed and folded and refolded—the twin-sized sheets with a faded strawberry print. Kerry moved back into the laundry room and whispered and whispered—*I'm back I'm back do you hear me hear me*—until her throat was raw to whoever, whomever was listening.

AT THE STATION, Kerry's bus is late. Over an hour—delayed by the January snow. Kerry chews on her bottom lip. She checks her watch: 8:13, 8:13, 8:14…. At 8:30, she stands up, puts her hands in her pockets, and pulls out a pack of Life Savers. She rolls the candy between her fingers until her knuckles ache. Then, she switches hands and does it again. Kerry has never been to Florida. Never. "This is a mistake," she says. Kerry grabs her suitcase and starts to walk out of the station as the bus pulls into her pathway. "This is a mistake," she says when boarding. Her seat is next to the window. She shares her row with a man from St. Cloud who once played hockey for the University's Huskies but lost his scholarship when his grades went to shit. "My grades went to shit," he says. "When Mom got sick, who could care." And then at the very first stop in Mora, Minnesota—population 2,436—the televisions, cornered in the corners of the station where people ushered through for bathroom breaks, bitter coffee, and easy food, suddenly synced with news outlets across the globe to broadcast the same, the same, the same. This just in. This is a mistake.

SO WHEN THEY watched the spaceship explode, when it burst in the Florida sky, disintegrated over the Atlantic Ocean while crowds gathered for the countdown, while news stations went live, while children and their teachers watched in auditoriums across the country to celebrate one of their own who boarded the ship with an apple for luck—73 seconds, then gasses, then fire so explosive, so hot it turned metal, turns bodies into dust that disappeared into the atmosphere—Kerry stood up and screamed, "I'm sorry! I'm sorry! Forgive me!"

EVENTUALLY, SHE WOULD get home—as would we all—and unpack our shirts as quickly as we could: shirt, shorts, shirt, shorts. Brushing the sugary candy out of our teeth, the university hockey player off the roster—top right, bottom left. Wash, rinse, repeat, as the instructions instruct. The recipe, the rules. Wash, rinse, repeat—prescribed prescription. *I'm back I'm back!* But by then, it didn't matter. It is already too late.

AND SO IT goes. The gas station, the cans of Dr. Peppers, the brown jacket with frayed cuffs, hockey players from the north en route to the south, the calls to sisters in Florida. "When are you coming?" she asks. And Kerry responds, "I can't. I'm sorry. Forgive me." Now part of the routine, too. And then so it goes. For gracious, merciful, benevolent God in heaven, so it goes.

⌐⌐

ELIZABETH CONWAY has her MFA from the University of Montana. Her fiction has been a finalist in *Glimmer Train's* Open Fiction contest, *Reed Magazine's* John Steinbeck Award, and the *Southeast Review's* World's Best Short-Short Story Contest. Most recently, her work can be found in the *Weird Sisters: Lilac City Fairy Tales* anthology by Scabland Books, and the *Blue Earth Review*. Elizabeth works, writes, and plays out of Missoula, Montana.

9

Fact of Nature

D. E. HARDY

You could think of it as an evolutionary advancement. Steelheads can spawn multiple times, whereas their salmon kin buck their way upstream only once. It's a good thing: the average steelhead dad swims out to the big ocean for a couple of months, has a time of it, then comes back to his small hometown river to make a family. Repeat. Repeat. Repeat. Higher chance his DNA survives. Nobody holds it against him. Nobody gets cross. Nobody gets pissed at you for sticking up for him. He's your dad, and it's okay to like your dad even though he left. It's not bad to have multiple families. It's the whole point.

You could think of it as an act of optimism. A steelhead dad doesn't need to stick around because he trusts his kids to handle themselves. A small-time river's not so big that a young fry can't figure things out. You hatch; you swim. That's it. Somebody will be around to show you how to catch a baseball or fix the chain on a bike or mow a lawn. That's what an ecosystem is for.

You could think of it as a simple fact of nature. Steelheads don't know who their half-siblings are, so you never know when you might swim by each other. It must happen all the time. They might live near you or maybe one river over. They might look exactly like you with the same square jaw, the same hair so blond it's silver. Somebody might say they saw you at the Kmart off M-39 even though you were at Little League. Somebody else might swear they saw you at the Pizza Hut buffet because the kid used cottage cheese as a salad dressing, just like you do. You might go to the county youth fair with your mom and wander toward the carnival games. You might come across a booth with a giant trout marquee where a kid that looks like you stands next to a lady your dad used to work with, playing one of those fishing games where you try to catch wooden fish with a magnet, you grabbing your mom's wrist, saying, *Please don't,* she stopping cold, saying, *That son of a bitch.*

***

D. E. HARDY'S work has appeared in *X-R-A-Y Magazine, Lost Balloon, Flashback Fiction, New World Writing,* among others. Her work has been nominated for a *Pushcart Prize* and anthologized in *Best Small Fictions 2022* and

Best Microfictions 2023. She lives in the San Francisco Bay Area and can be followed on Twitter @dehardywriter and at www.dehardywriter.com.

10

Autopsy

AIMEE LABRIE

It wasn't a date exactly. He said, "Do you want to see a dead body?"

I said yes.

I would have done anything to spend time with him. I was a secretary for the medical school, and he was a student. He liked to drop by and talk to me between his neurology lecture and gross anatomy.

It could even be that I suggested it. Maybe he was leaning on my desk between classes, talking about anatomy lab. Armen—he had curly dark hair and a prominent Adam's apple that I wanted to press my mouth against.

Maybe I said I wanted to see it—the body.

He led me to the lower level of the building. I didn't even know I was working in a place that housed cadavers. He gave me a blue gown to put on. He tied the strings gently in the back, careful not to touch me.

I could feel him behind me, his breath on my neck.

He said, "Are you ready?" I nodded. The room was filled with what looked like silver operating tables. He pressed a button. The table vibrated, made a humming sound. Two slits opened, and the body rose from underneath, covered in a plastic sheet.

The smell of formaldehyde—I knew it from my own high school anatomy class when we dissected alley cats. The pungent, sharp smell ballooned inside of me, and went straight to my temple, with a needle-like pain.

I took two steps backward. He caught my elbow. "Are you sure you want to see this?"

"I'm fine," I said.

He pulled back the sheet. A woman, skin ashy gray. What was left of the skin. You couldn't even really think of her as an intact body. They were in week 12 of dissection.

I stepped back when I saw her face. It was the lady outside of the Broad and Snyder subway stop, her skin tanned from being outside, wriggly hand-drawn tattoos snaking up her arms like bracelets. She always held the free paper, *Streetwise*.

Every once in a while, I would buy a copy. That meant giving her a dollar and taking the paper down into the subway with me and then leaving it on a bench in case she ventured down there to get it again. Two for the price of one.

On other days (most days), I would cross the street to avoid her, take the subway entrance on the wrong side of the street so I didn't have to face her, teeth missing, stumps in her head, the un-prettiness of homeless people, the way they are vulnerable to everything.

I never caught her name, but in my head, I thought of her as Madge. Madge had a series of wigs she wore—a wild, burly one like Harpo Marx, and another one with long hair and bangs; disconcerting to see her from behind with the shiny hair falling down her back, and then to have her turn, a face shriveled up like a dried apple. I presumed that she did all kinds of things for money, that the costumes were part of the way she made her living. It reminded me of a jock in high school who I overheard saying that toothless women give the best blowies. Nice and smooth, he said.

"You see this?" Armen said. "We had to peel back three layers of fat to get inside." He pointed to her lungs. "Dark spots," he said. "She was a smoker." He turned to the chest cavity with its row of rib bones cut across the sternum so they could see inside. He picked up the heart, moved it around in his hands. "Do you want to hold it?" His voice joking, even as he held it out to me.

It was much smaller than I expected. It looked like a decaying avocado.

Armen took her hand in his. I thought he was pretending to hold it, like they were on a date, but he turned the wrist to show her tendons through the skin. "See this?" With his gloved hand, he identified a muscle, pointed, then pulled. Her fingers wiggled. "She's waving to you," he said.

I took shallow breaths, pretending to be interested in the white tangle of her intestines. "Do you know her name?"

He explained that most of the donors were either the homeless or the unidentified.

I nodded my head. It felt strange on my neck, loose, like it could fall off any second and roll across the floor. The woman had probably gotten money for donating her body, money she spent on food or clothes or wigs.

"We're doing the brain next." He brought me to the front of the body. This seemed better, away from the carnage of the cut skin, the places on her arms where they practiced giving stitches, the split in her abdomen where they sawed away to learn about her uterus. Her eyes were shut, her face untouched. Long black eyelashes, thin lips, a broad nose. She had dots in her ears where her earrings had been removed. "Look at this," Armen said. He pulled at the top of her head, and her skull opened up, like a jar.

I stayed where I was. I did not want to see the gray curves of her brain. "What happens after?" I asked.

"After?" he replaced the piece of her skull, smoothed her hair back into place.

"When you're done."

He bent close to her body, fingers tapping against her rib cage. He had more he wanted to show me, but there was a ringing in my ears now. It occurred to me that he didn't have the same feelings that I did. She was just part of his lesson.

"I'm not sure what happens to her after." He looked at me and smiled. "We haven't gotten to that part yet."

AIMEE LABRIE'S short stories have appeared in *The Minnesota Review, Iron Horse Literary Review, StoryQuarterly, Cimarron Review, Pleiades, Beloit Fiction Journal, Permafrost Magazine,*

and others. Her second collection of short stories, *Rage and Other Cages*, was published by Leapfrog Press in September 2023. In 2007, her short story collection, *Wonderful Girl*, was awarded the Katherine Anne Porter Prize in Short Fiction and published in a small print run (University of North Texas Press). Her short fiction has been nominated three times for the Pushcart Prize. In 2012 she won first place in the Zoetrope: All-Story's Short Fiction Competition.

11

Submission Guidelines

TONEE MOLL

We want your very best work! Writers at every stage of their career are encouraged to submit, but we want writing that goes hard. We want the stuff that punches us right in the ear, perforating the drum in such a way it prevents us from swimming that whole haunted summer, despite the heat, despite the ghost of missing out.

We want work of any genre that reminds us of the way it felt when we first fell in love with literature, that sensation we got when we first realized that this feeling we had for Zak wasn't just admiration or jealousy, but that teenage cocktail of lust and hope that bodies can be bound together into something sweet, something sweat, something important and worth remembering. But his grandfather had just passed earlier that June, and we could tell it hit Zak hard the morning that we showed up on his doorstep. We were still on antibiotic eardrops and under orders to avoid blowing our nose, and he answered with an open, loose Hawaiian shirt, and the singe across the crest of our cheeks explained that desire had found its way back into our body for the first time in weeks, but after that initial flush, we noticed there was something off about him, that he wasn't the charismatic skate kid we'd watched practice kickflips for months, as we sat on the curb with our own deck rolling back and forth beneath our feet. With the late morning sun bending through the glass outer door and onto his bare chest, we realized that he looked hollow—no, not exactly hollow, but, like, separate? A step removed from the moment? Not the person we saw, but like someone behind a windshield, operating his body.

Prose writers, send us 500-4,500 words of absolute heat, keeping in mind that the symbolic connection between "heat" and foundational summer crushes is too obvious, so you'll need to talk your way into some other sort of figurative framework. Like, do you remember Deana Carter? We think of that song when we think of that summer. And, listen, we know country music is outside of the aesthetic of whatever this is, but hear us out: yes, "Strawberry Wine" does dip its feet into the clichés of summer and heat imagery, but Carter does it in a way that gives it a little ya' know, like, a little turn, a little zing. When she considers the ephemeral nature of the summertime, what is named is "September's arrival" rather than summer's passing. This is season as a sort of haunting. As for "heat," here too, Carter subverts expectations. One might expect it to arrive in the sun, summer, or bodies, but she offers instead the "hot July moon" as the only witness to her clandestine summer passion, and even though we had started listening to pop punk that year, the country song was buzzing from an alarm-clock radio flipped on for white noise to mask hard breathing. Slipping under the covers alone, the thought of sunlight on Zak's chest rushing forward, we gently ground ourself against a pillow until nearly breathless, until having the dangerous idea to call him from the phone it took months to convince our parents to install in the room, then hanging up the moment that he answered.

For poets, send us up to five pages of poetry in any style: we don't care if it's free verse, fixed verse, or even experimental—as long as it BLEEDS. We want to feel it, like a sunburn. Like a knee scoured on blacktop in the summer, a Nevada summer, a couple of weeks after we'd seen Zak at his front door. We had been coming to that parking lot of the "other mall," where everyone skated after school and before work, each of us picking up or setting down fountain lemonades that the Greek pizza joint on the corner would usually let us steal, despite our obviousness, when we asked for free water cups. We want poetry that BLOOMS, the way we did at first, when we saw him squatting outside the driver's door of a faded Civic, our feelings rising as we recognized his profile there in the afternoon light and unfolding as we wondered why he was crouching like that, and whose car it was, and pausing briefly to chuckle at the thought that it must have been because he was hiding a beer, maybe smoking up.

We want poems that shift our tenses. We want poems that burst into full color when we see Zak slip his thumb deep into the mouth—no, down the throat—of that rawboned emo guy who works at Spencer's in the "good mall," and Zak is looking at him, and he's looking at the ceiling of his car, and that's when we put together that Zak's hands must be in his lap, and we can tell that they are moving fast, and Zak's doing this thing where he's trying to be attentive to the guy he's getting off, but he's also glancing around, making sure they don't get caught, so at first we don't think he sees us here, watching them. Then he turns his head and looks us right in the eye, as though he sensed us there, and for a breath's length, his face shows panic as he realizes someone is watching him, until he registers that it's us, and, as if we were in on it all, smiles: a disorderly, charming smirk.

We smile back, eventually and also briefly, because we don't know what else to do, then look down, pick up our lemonade cup off of the curb, and kick our deck forward to ride the opposite direction, away from asphalt lot.

For some reason we still can't pinpoint, the most vivid memory left today isn't the smile, but the paired rasp of wheels on concrete, the rhythmic click as we slid along the sidewalk, away from longing.

No simultaneous submissions.

TONEE MOLL is a queer writer and educator. Their work has appeared in *Poet Lore*, *jubilat*, *Little Patuxent Review*, and more. Tonee is a PhD candidate in English and holds an MFA in creative writing & publishing arts. Their debut memoir, *Out of Step*, won a 2018 Lambda Literary Award and the 2017 Nonfiction Prize. Their latest collection of poems, *You Cannot Save Here*, won the 2022 Jean Feldman Poetry Prize. It is available now from Washington Writers' Publishing House.

12

Into the White

GILLIAN O'SHAUGHNESSY

The wolves are out again. I can hear them, their hollow wails in the pines, slicing through a storm of snow. It's my turn to get the wood in. It was my turn last night and the night before and the night before that, too, but Father says I'm mistaken. He's so careful not to slur his words, I know not to argue. Instead, I offer a skinny smile. He says I look like I'm fed on lemons and sugar, and he'll fix my face if I don't fix it first.

I pull on the old boots he keeps by the door. They're always too big, no matter how tight I pull the laces and wind the ends around and around my ankles. They used to be his best boots, buffed brown leather, the colour of honey. They turned black with age and damp and rot. My father's eyes were brown once too.

The shed is 50 steps away exactly in the kind of snow when you take into account the weight of the wood sled. I know because I've counted. It's easy to miss the shed in bad weather, and there's nothing past it but the forest. I'm cold, and I can feel watchful gazes trace my path as I walk. Or maybe I imagine them. I can see thin skeins of frosted breath rise through the trees in the dark, or maybe it's only the mist. I go step by step. I don't lose count even as the storm begins to settle.

At the woodshed, the old door lurches on its hinges like a drunk. I feel for the axe near the edge of the doorframe, even before I turn the light on. The sleet and the wind whistle through cracks in the window and a gap in the wall. The bare bulb sways on its frayed cord, and the wood is wet and fetid. I can't recall when we last stacked it neatly. That was always Mama's job.

I chop the logs fast. Father says I'm stronger than I look and fierce. It used to make me proud when he said that, I don't remember why. I pile up the sled and go to put the axe back in its place. In the doorway, between me and the house, stands a thin grey wolf. Still as winter. Looking at me with a steady gaze, its head held low. Fear clutches at my gut like a punch.

Father always said to run if you can from a fight, but if you can't, go in early and hard, use your fists and teeth and everything. Be wild like an animal, and you'll win, sure as anything. I used to believe him. The grey wolf glitters sharp under the glow of a luminous moon. I put down my axe and step into the white. Reach out my hand. I don't remember why.

GILLIAN O'SHAUGHNESSY is a short fiction writer from Fremantle in Western Australia. She has work in *Jellyfish*

Review, Splonk, SmokeLong Quarterly, and the inaugural *Fractured Lit Anthology*, among others. Find her online @GillOshaughness or gillianoshaughnessy.com.

13

Galgalim

ERIC PAHRE

It is not an air raid. Above the city's steepled church-tops the two planes break from the clouds. Sunlit rain begins to trickle down, and then the smell from wet city streets. The clock tower strikes a warning.

"Judita, you had best head home before they begin," says the young man selling apricots. He is much younger than her, and she wonders—if she'd been a younger mother—if her eldest would now look something like him.

"Why would I tire myself out hurrying already?" says Judita.

The shoppers point at the coming airplanes, but after all this time, they no longer duck underneath the store's racks or brace themselves in one of the old plaza's archways.

There's that odd murmuring, of the townspeople, of which will win this time?

Judita doesn't hide because nobody else is hiding. Of course, they won't fire at any of the people on the ground. Already the pilots above are likely saluting one another and grinning at their chance to take another round.

Up there, the airplanes shine like coins, wings tipped at angles into the wet sunlight. Engines and propellers chatter. Davit, if he were here, would tell her the engines' names with some pride, machines named after some bird of prey. When the red plane finds its way out from the sunlight, she sees faintly the many-colored patterning along its oval wings and knows that it is the machine named *Pierrougia*.

Pierrougia tips a wing at the approaching pilot; a salute. Then it is the opening of both planes' Vickers guns, the rolling of the shapes in their joust with engines bickering on, then both are away back into the clouds, untouched.

Davit said once, lying on the grass and tearing at a dandelion, that the new airplanes can dodge raindrops if they so choose. But *Pierrougia* and the other machines are old and must take the warm water and contend with rusting and their pilots' slipping on the wing when it is time to dismount.

Up in their apartment, Judita finds her father and her daughter.

Simon is there in the kitchen with the girl balanced on his side, his granddaughter fallen asleep on an old shoulder. The barely-damp breeze pulls at a hanging shirt and carries with it that same lasting smell of fallen rain, and the man shifts slightly to the warm sound of a folk dance on the living room radio.

It is as though Simon is a new father himself: no longer Judita's but a doting man, smiling with the sleeping girl, reborn in this way. Judita finds a large wicker basket at the foot of a cupboard, and begins corralling items, quickly.

"Still in some hurry?" Simon whispers.

"How was it today?" Judita says, and her father just looks down at the sleeping girl and raises his eyebrows, nodding.

Judita looks at her daughter. Why does she somehow feel like a grandmother and not a mother—and how many gray hairs will her girl find when she begins to truly see? Will it be the handful, now, or the head of a withered mother who cannot run with her and speaks with the voice of Judita's own mother?

Judita ducks low to reach out and close the window, and there are the planes again up high: *Pierrougia*'s red hull is blazing with stars and in a wheeling whirlwind, passes. The foes' guns begin to roar again.

Pierrougia weaves through it all and finds its way to double back, opening fire, and there is that sharp clang of some stray bullet striking the adversary's hull. Both planes vanish again, behind the clocktower. Rain, again, briefly falls. Judita smells petrol. Her daughter sleeps through it all, nestled into her grandfather's shoulder as he sways.

Judita is in the rocky field not far from the city, the sun shining through the clouds. The scattered boulders are damp: pebbles, gleaming. She opens her basket and unfurls the blanket atop smooth grass.

Judita arranges the pieces of food, pouring an extra glass of wine at the picnic site. If she sets it all up like this, with everything in order, then he will know just where to land.

The machines do return: *Pierrougia*, at tilt. Turning and turning, rising like a merlin in a high thermal. The sound of engines is the only thing; then guns that fire again, from both sides, and the adversary is totaled with the flames bursting across its metal span as it twists away down into the wooded marshland. *Pierrougia* tips a wing in salute again.

But the red, starry airplane has taken it, too, and then Judita's stomach has a slight turn as always as she sees the plane wilting from the sky and trailing black smoke.

Pierrougia comes down hard, scraping to a stop at the rocky edge of the field, the pilot clambering from the airplane as flames begin to bloom at its propellor, him popping up the cockpit's glass and sliding down the wet wing. The pilot, leather-capped, throws his shattered goggles into the wreckage.

Pierrougia burns again. The pilot wanders toward Judita's picnic, stretching his arms and stuffing gloves into his pockets. Steam rises from the metal of his harness that he just then begins to notice, and he unfastens his belt, the heavy pieces falling away to hiss in the spring grass.

He sits, and she hands him wine, saying, "Are you all right this time?"

His eyes are great and cloud-filled, ringed by the bruises of heavy goggles.

"Well enough, he says." They drink.

"You nearly woke her up this time, fighting so close to the city," Judita says. "You could fight somewhere else next time."

Davit is famished and digs into the plate of bread and cheese, thumbing the pit from an apricot. He looks older, there, but Judita must remind herself that he has gotten older since they were married.

"If we fought up in the mountains or down across the marshland," Davit says, "who would see us?"

ERIC PAHRE is a writer from Illinois. He completed his MFA at the University of South Carolina and now lives in Chicago, where he is a PhD. student in the Program for Writers at the University of Illinois at Chicago.

14

Background

K. A. POLZIN

I didn't have any theater experience, but when I saw the ad for background actors for a local play, I thought it sounded fun: wear a costume, stand in the back, get paid $60 a show. I heard they were taking whoever fit the costumes.

The play, it turned out, was outside, in Greenstone Park. It was one of those new immersive theater experiences. I had to pretend to be selling shoes to a customer—also a background actor. We just pantomimed the thing to add atmosphere but not detract from the main cast, who roamed the park while little groups of audience members followed them. Different scenes took place in different parts of the park, and the audience could pick what part of the story they wanted to follow.

The first few nights, I pantomimed shoe sales with Terri: I'd show her different shoes, she'd ooh and aah, or shake her head, or whatever. There was always a stream of people walking by, watching. Then one night, a woman from the audience walked over, picked up a shoe, and tried it on. This was allowed. We were supposed to go with it. I smiled at her obsequiously—I was getting into this acting thing—then leaned down and fastened the strap of her shoe.

She turned her foot side to side, took a look at it in the shoe. "What do you think?" she said.

This was not allowed. Audience members could only speak if an actor spoke to them, and Terri and I weren't allowed to speak at all. But, I thought, who's gonna know?

"Pretty snazzy," I said.

She smiled, pleased to be part of the play. "I'll take them," she said.

Our "set" was just a few racks with some shoes that it looked like the props department had gotten from the thrift store. I had to improvise. "I'll put them on your tab," I said, something I remembered from old movies.

She nodded at me demurely, as though she was in the same movie, then slipped on her flats, stood, and meandered off, carrying the shoes by their straps like someone at the beach.

Terri looked at me like *what the fuck*, and I just shrugged.

But I'd broken my maiden. I'd seen how fun this acting thing could be. Now I wanted more lines.

So when audience members strolled by, taking in the pantomimed sideshow, I'd say hello, invite them into our "shop." They'd browse the shoes, chat with me, all the while looking a bit unsure, no doubt wondering, *Is this part of the story?* You see, they were always in search of the story, never quite sure which actors to follow, which were going to start speaking.

There was an apothecary on one side of us, a bookshop on the other. Brandon, the bookseller, saw what was going on. He could've been uptight, turned us in, but instead, he gave us a conspiratorial grin, nodded his head yes. Pretty soon I saw him chatting with the audience, bringing them into the shop, unshelving the thrift store books, and handing them to his "customers."

Esther in the apothecary looked confused, asked, "Are we supposed to be doing that?"

"Not technically."

She wrinkled her nose. But I didn't think she'd say anything.

The shoe-selling was fun, but, I thought. *I want to be part of the story.*

I made a plan with Brandon. We wrote some dialogue for ourselves. When customers came in, after showing them our wares, we'd whisper to them, *The king is dead. That is an impostor.* This drew a lot of excited looks. I could tell our audience thought they'd uncovered the big secret of the play, that they'd done it by being clever and exploring all the little shops.

I still think what happened next was a good thing. It only made the play better, more immersive. If there was a problem, it was because the actors, the professional ones, wouldn't listen to the audience, couldn't evolve along with the play.

What happened was this: the king and his retinue were just across from our shop in the Rose Garden performing their usual scene, same as every night, when an audience member called out, "The king is dead! That is an impostor!" The actor-king was caught off guard, looked unsure for a moment, but to his credit, he stayed in character and barked, "Apprehend that man." Two guards grabbed the man by the arms, theatrical-style, which it was clear was great fun for him. Others wanted in.

"The king is dead! That is an impostor!" someone else called. Then, from elsewhere: "He's an impostor! Impostor!"

It was full-on audience improv. And they were loving it. Only the actors were having a problem. "No, I…," the king said, then ran out of words. A stage manager, uncostumed and holding a walkie, stepped out from behind a tree. I could see things were devolving.

Then suddenly, I just knew. I strode out of my shop, holding my head up imperiously, walked straight up to the king (real name: Jerry), and removed his crown. As I placed it on my head, in my best king voice, I announced, "I am Gerald, brother of the late King, true successor to the throne!"

There were cheers all around and some huzzahs, at least from the audience. Jerry looked miffed. But he only had himself to blame.

I gave a short speech to my subjects while the stage manager was alerting Security. I bowed before they escorted me away.

PEOPLE LOVED THE play that night; there are still seven five-star reviews on Yelp from that performance.

Of course, I was fired. As was Brandon.

Terri is the shoe seller in the shop now. Good for her.

I get it now: it's not just the acting that I crave; it's the giving in, the letting it happen, whatever the moment wants. Something Jerry will never understand.

K. A. POLZIN is a writer and cartoonist whose stories have appeared (or are forthcoming) in *Subtropics*, *EVENT*, *Lunch Ticket*, and elsewhere, and whose short humor and cartoons have appeared in *McSweeney's Internet Tendency*, *Narrative Magazine*, and *Electric Literature*.

15

When We're Empty of What
We Are Designed to Hold

QUINN RENNERFELDT

One Sunday morning, I wake up to discover that both of my daughters have turned into birds. The younger—a tow-headed chatterbox, always sidling up to me when I baked, eager to add a spice of her choosing to the recipe—is a great blue heron stalking around the kitchen on reedy legs, probing the drain for fish. The oldest—wise beyond her years, sarcastic, and often mired in thought—is a regal swan, aloof in the living room. I discover our dog on the landing, covered in piss, shaking and whining. My husband has left coffee on my nightstand, still steaming, beside a note: gone for bird seed.

I cup my mug in both hands, letting the heat leach through the ceramic clay into my palms. The pain of the heat centers me. I do not know what to do with two bird-daughters, but instinct tells me I need to be fully human right now. Grounded, present. Other new-agey aphorisms. I consider doing child's pose, but the fetal position feels more appropriate. I spend a good half-hour curled like a shell on the floating island of my mattress. I breathe like unpredictable surf, doing its in-out thing. The featherlight clicks of talons on the linoleum floor seep under the door, sending panic into my brain. Meditation feels useless when surrounded by girl-bird sounds.

BEFORE TODAY, I would've considered myself an amateur birder. I logged bird sightings into my Audobon app as I walked through the park. Got a little thrill when spotting red or blue plumage. But it's clear I'm out of my element. It's 9:30a.m., and I realize it's well past breakfast time. I cautiously peer around the door frame into the kitchen. My heron-daughter is quiet, perched on one leg; she has given up her attempt to forage in the disposal. She studies me with a flat yellow eye. Her beak is the shape of a blade. I sidle up to the cabinet, back pressed to the door, and slowly creep a hand in to grab a bag of bonito flakes. I dump them out onto a plastic fox plate from her toddler years, a nostalgic place setting I could never part with. The plate she used to lick the remnants of cake crumbs from on her birthdays. I set it on the floor and sneak out of the room. I can't witness this new avian form of eating, with no tongue or teeth in sight. I tiptoe to the living room against the soundtrack of keratin blades pecking plastic.

Swan-daughter is patiently preening, nuzzling through her white feathers, waterproofing her wings, even though the best I could offer her at this moment is a baby pool that has collected dead leaves in our backyard. Or she could join the bird-shaped paddle boats on Stowe Lake, where her glorious plumage would steal the show.

I SLOWLY UNVEIL a piece of bread stolen from the kitchen before I flee. I shred it into small mouthfuls and scatter it in front of me, breathing quietly as she waddles over to eat. She is dainty and careful in her consumption; she doesn't look at me, but I can tell she is as aware of my presence as I am of hers. Still studious in her new form. I remember reading, once, how aggressive swans are about protecting their nests. One man is rumored to have drowned in a swan attack, a merciless mother beating him relentlessly when he waded too close to her hidden eggs. I am keenly aware of swan-daughter's sturdy frame, her long, muscular neck. The white feathers a false sense of security, my swan-daughter dressed as sur-render. Even as a human, she outgrew physical intimacy quickly; hugs and cuddles turned into squirming away, a shoulder lent for a quick embrace while still leaving bodily space between us. I simultaneously want to stroke her back and flee to "buy bird seed."

BUT I'M NAILED in place, watching my love change shape into something interspatial, interspecies. My heart downy as velvet. Heron-daughter approaches us both. We stand as a trio, observing one another, balanced like a three-legged stool. I outstretch my hands, crumbed from the bread. I'm reminded of religious iconog-raphy, minus the gentle dove or goldfinch. I close my eyes. The funk of feathers fills my nose. I can feel their mouths investigating my palms, equally cautious. All of us, navigating this new relational space. They are moving through the world as reimagined creatures, divine. Leaving me—and my arms, bare of all but freckles and blonde hairs—behind.

As though without thinking, I open the largest window of the living room. Swan-daughter has to bow her head slightly to get through, but she is quickly gone, as I always feared. Her leaving, in the moment, takes on a quality of quartz; held at one angle, it is opaque, a punctureless grief. Tilted, it becomes clear, something that welcomes and reflects the light.

Heron-daughter perches on the sill for a moment, as though considering how I might be feeling. My youngest, my shadow, who would part parents at the playground like Moses parting the sea, always looking for me. She cocks her bird-head in my direction. Her expression reads as apology, or perhaps I'm anthropomorphizing. Then she stretches neck, body, leg, and wing, a giant being. She swoops down the street. Turns the corner where I can no longer see her. I shuffle to the door of their shared room, now childless. A few down feathers nested in the blankets. I plant my feet on the floor and then my palms. Knees perched on the back of my arms, I dip my head, complete a crow pose.

AFTER A TIME, the doorbell rings. I expect a bird-daughter returned, or perhaps a husband, replete with seeds. But when I open the door, I am greeted by a big blue egg, three feet in height. We consider each other in silence for a moment, and then I invite her inside.

QUINN RENNERFELDT is a queer parent, partner, and poetry/prose writer earning her MFA at San Francisco State University. Their heart is equally wed to the Pacific Ocean and the Rocky Mountains. Her work can be found in *Cleaver*, *Mom Egg Review*, *SAND*, and elsewhere, and is forthcoming in *A Velvet Giant* and *Salamander*. They are the recipient of the 2022 Harold Taylor Prize, sponsored by the Academy of American Poets. Her chapbook *Sea Glass Catastrophe* was released in 2020 by *Francis House Press*. They are the editor-in-chief of *Fourteen Hills*, a graduate-run literary journal with SFSU.

16

Adrift

KIM STEUTERMANN ROGERS

It was the year the flood washed a parade of homes downriver. They called it a rain bomb. Kate's home was fourth. She followed three other women, unable or unwilling to leave their homes that once lined the largest river on their tropical island. Kate tried her phone, but no calls connected.

Aunty Lani, from the house ahead of her, tossed Kate a rope, and that's how the four women tied their homes, their lives, their fates together. What a sight. Four houses, all shades of green, headed for a crescent-shaped bay backdropped by lush fluted mountains sliced with waterfalls. Oh, the waterfalls. So many that they looked like icing dribbling down the creases of a pound cake.

There was food and water. Everyone packed disaster kits these days. Everyone filled their bathtubs whenever sirens alerted a pending natural disaster. Everyone knew the disasters were coming more and more often. It used to be hurricanes or tsunamis, but with warming temperatures, extreme flooding had become a more deadly disaster.

It stopped raining by evening. At dusk, frogs climbed onto the women's decks. Frogs by the dozen, frogs crawling on top of other frogs, frogs seeking rescue and sending the women onto their roofs at sunset, as a full moon rose over the eastern sky, painting it a postapocalyptic orange-gold.

For dinner, Jodi shared a vegetarian lasagna she'd made the day before with taro leaves and vegan cheese. Kate made a salad from the bag of mixed greens, her last from her ex-girlfriend, the farmer. The women shuttled everything, one to the other, in baskets they hooked to the ropes connecting them.

"Like dessert?" Aunty asked and passed around banana bread with macadamia nuts, the bananas and nuts she grew in what was once her backyard. Stephanie was the practical one. She tossed everyone a lime and said they were good for washing your hands. "Armpits, too."

At ten o'clock, a phone pinged, and everyone thought they'd floated into cell phone range, but it was just Jodi's alarm, a reminder to take melatonin before bed. Instead, Aunty passed around a bottle of Patron. "I was saving it," she said. "But I figure this is as special as it gets." Stephanie went inside her house and returned with tortilla chips and salsa. "Good to have something on the stomach," she said.

No one slept that night, and Kate learned their stories, piecemeal, relayed like the old game of telephone. Aunty was going through a divorce, or not, she couldn't decide. Her husband spent most of his time fishing or racing outrigger canoes, his first love the ocean, a cliché if there ever was one. Stephanie had just lost her dog to cancer. Jodi was a cancer survivor—breast. And, Kate, recently split from her long-time girlfriend, her lease expiring, trying to figure out her next move. As a seasonal field biologist, Kate couldn't afford to live alone in Hawaii.

Kate tried her phone again. No bars.
No one asked the question that was on everyone's mind.

When the moon started to arc for the horizon, Aunty ran fishing lines between the houses and baited the hooks with frogs. She'd learned a few tricks from her fisherman husband, she said. With any luck, she'd cube up an aweoweo and make poke for breakfast. "I've got scallions," Kate said, another leftover from her girlfriend. Jodi didn't eat fish, not after the baby seal died when it snagged a fish off a fisherman's line, swallowing the hook, too. But she offered chili pepper water.

Just before the moon dropped out of sight, Kate heard the sound of a whoosh and felt a spray of droplets coat her body. A pungent smell lodged in the back of her throat, and she could just make out a humpback whale, a bloom of red expanding around it. As the women watched, another whale one-third the size surfaced. They listened as they heard the whale calf take its first breath. They watched as it nudged its mother's side and wrapped its long slender tongue around a teat extending from its mother's belly. The whales rolled around on the water's surface, sounding shortly after sunrise.

Kate could barely see the island, their flotilla having drifted far offshore, but she could see the look on every woman's face. "That deserves more Patron," Aunty said and sent the tequila around again.

Before they could check the fishing lines and think about making breakfast, they heard it. Whoop. Whoop. Whoop. The women looked up, their hair blowing in the turbulence of the helicopter's blades. But not a single one stood.

KIM STEUTERMANN ROGERS lives with her husband and sixteen-year-old dog Lulu in Hawaii. Her essay, "Following the Albatross Home," was recognized as Notable in *Best American Travel Writing*. Her journalism has published in *National Geographic*, *Audubon*, and *Smithsonian*, and her prose in *Atticus Review*, *CHEAP POP*, *Hippocampus*, and elsewhere. She was awarded residencies at Storyknife Writers Retreat in Alaska in 2016 and 2021 and Dorland Mountain Arts in 2022. Find her @kimsrogers.

17

Two Cops Come to the Door

ARTHUR RUSSELL

Yes, I saw something. I was making my regular Friday night sauce-and-cheese sandwich. It's like pizza on an Italian bread. When I went to junior high, Fred's, the pizza place, sold sauce-and-cheese sandwiches at lunch hour for a dollar; came with a Coke, but now I like to have it with a glass of wine. Took nearly 40 years to realize I could make it at home. It's so delicious. I don't even bother to make it with excellent quality mozzarella, and I use bottled sauce, but I also drizzle olive oil on the bread and Pecorino Romano. It's really better than pizza because the bread holds so much sauce you rarely, if ever, put it down between bites. First of all, it's warm in your hand, and second, you're going to want to keep eating.

So, I was by the window, which is by the toaster oven, which is where I make my sandwiches, when I saw Alan Hemshaw running through the backyard. Actually, it was the ginger cat running away from Hemshaw that triggered the motion detector that triggered the floodlights, and a few seconds later, Hemshaw came through. I didn't see his face, but I recognized him by his gait. You can recognize a person by their gait more reliably at 30 yards than any other measure. That's my theory, anyway, never read about it anywhere. You guys want coffee?

December, it gets dark by 4:30, and the floodlights are very spooky, when they shine up into the pine tree especially. Did you ever hear of David Crosby, from Crosby, Stills & Nash? You're probably not old enough. Anyway, Hemshaw has this tall man's gait; I was gonna say he reminds me of Neil Young, but then I realized, not really. He's a tall, wide-shouldered, leaning forward kind of guy, looks like he's eating at the sink even when he's at a wedding, and he goes running by. I figured he got into it with Jeanette Fiero, the daughter of the retired school superintendent, Jim Fiero. Jim Fiero used to live two doors down from me, and when Jeanette married, she lived up the block the other way, and Hemshaw and me, we'd gone to Nutley High together; we'd meet at the Tick Tock Diner after dates on Saturday nights to compare notes, which is to say to brag, which is to say we lied, so I was very familiar with Hemshaw's attitudes toward women generally, and to Jeanette Fiero specifically, which is to say, basically Neanderthal. He'd been up Jeanette Fiero's leggings for 38 years, at least aspiration-ally, plus one stint before she got married and another last year after she got divorced. You sure you don't want some coffee? I've got crumb cake from Styertowne.

Last year, July Fourth weekend, I saw them packing up her RAV4. I'm pretty certain they were headed to the Shore; at least, when I see someone in a straw hat sliding a beach chair in the back of a Rav 4, that's what I think. I figured they're together again, and it had this offbeat, whaddya know vibe as far as I'm concerned, going back, as I say, to Nutley High. In high school, you'd know kids like Denise Santangelo and Dean Mercuris were going to get married the summer after graduation, and now they have grandkids like a deck of cards dropped on the living room floor, but there were others, the near misses, like Johnny Hamnett and Leslie Gaulin. They should have been a couple. Seriously, you'd see them in the hallway, and their heads were almost touching, and he wrote sonnets for her in the school paper, but she had something to prove and he was not the one she wanted to prove it to, which is a shame because she could've used a sensitive guy like that, and then there were the ones like Hemshaw and Jeanette Fiero, if you ever heard of slam dancing—probably before your time, too—that's how Hemshaw and Jeanette Fiero were, a total collision; so it was the ginger cat followed by Hemshaw; they crossed in front of my garage and through the pergola, back behind the Bernhardt's house, and, I do not believe, with all the fences and swimming pools, that you can even get to Rutgers Place through the backyards the way we did when we were kids, so I don't know where he went from there, but he was carrying a gun.

⌒⌒

In the late seventies and early eighties, ARTHUR RUSSELL studied fiction writing with Grace Paley, Raymond Carver, Tobias Wolff, and Allan Gurganus. Then, he got a job for which society would pay. Now, this.

18

Two Phenomena of Roughly Equal Importance

ROBERT SHAPARD

"The air on Mars—what there is of it—is leaking away," he said. "About half a pound a second sputtering into space. P-p-poof. Stripped away by solar winds." He was still in bed reading a NASA report in the Sunday *New York Times*.

It was a month since she'd moved into his house, more like a cottage, with a tiny yard. They'd dated in college, then hadn't seen each other in 10 years, happened to run into each other and remembered they liked each other. They were still learning how to talk to each other again.

"I got so stoned once," she said, "I lay on the floor and listened to the air squeaking in the vents all day. I thought I was on another planet. That was about a year after I met my jerk ex-husband."

He said *hmph,* waited a respectful five seconds, and put his iPad on the bedside table. "Mars's early atmosphere used to be like Earth's," he said, "but it didn't have a magnetic field like Earth's to hold it close. Now it's just wisps."

It wasn't working, she thought. Not that she was giving up.

In one motion, she slipped out of her exercise pants and panties, hopped up on the bed, and did a graceful half-roll toward him. "When I think of space, I think of the attic," she said. "I thought I heard something up there last night, did you?"

He liked to kiss the inside of her knee. She couldn't understand why but was patient about it.

In college, they'd had only three dates. On the third, he'd given her his engineering society pin and kissed her passionately. She said okay, weirdly pleased. He was not at all bad looking. But by the end of the evening, she was freaked out by the whole idea of the pin and gave it back when he took her home. He shook her hand, shook her hand. And they went on to other people. She'd liked him, though.

Now, in their early thirties, they were both divorced. She was childless, he had a daughter, who lived with his ex in a nearby city. He drove up, or flew up, every other weekend. He was an ecological engineer, worked for Boeing for a while, then went out on his own as a consultant. Lately, all he could get was low-level number crunching. Yesterday he was out at the lake evaluating a small dam, which he said beavers could have built better. She thought beavers were sweet, but weren't that important. Should he be competing with them? Before that, he had a job with a Bay Area steel mill, designing scrubbers for their smokestacks, but got laid off because the political winds had changed. That she could understand. Politics had been her life. She had a poly sci degree, from a good program, was a Democratic party girl (her words), then lost her way, marrying a conservative politician who cheated on her. Ever surrounded by ambition, she'd grown bitter and snarky. After the breakup, she had devised her own recovery program by temporarily working for an animal shelter and training for the Iron Man. She told friends it took an iron will not to bring home a pet from the animal control shelter. She didn't want to bond with it. Another breakup would be too much pain.

Now, even though they only had three dates in college, they were like old lovers, with new ground rules. They agreed not to talk about love. She let him know how she felt by patting him down before he jogged out to the park, a joke, to make sure he didn't have his engineering pin with him in case he wanted to kiss another woman. In response, he said, "It's just chemistry, mine's attracted to yours." He had a tin ear, but she could live with it.

Then why was she feeling so nettlesome this morning? His wife and daughter hadn't lived here for a year, but she felt like any minute, they'd come bustling in the door with groceries or after-school friends.

He had quit kissing her knee and started working his way up the inside of her thigh. "Is that supposed to drive me crazy?" she said, not meaning to sound snarky.

"No, it's to drive me crazy," he said. "Think of me as a spacecraft coming in to dock."

"I see," she said. "Are we going somewhere? In space, I mean?" She sighed, "I'm not trying to ruin your day, I just like to make sense of things."

"None of it makes sense without us," he said. "It makes sense if we want it to, you and me."

HE EASED BESIDE her, head even with hers, pinned her hand comfortably back, his fingers interlaced with hers.

"You sound like some poly sci theorist," she said.

He fell silent. She'd done it now. Again. Silenced him. His default was to not talk. She squeezed his hand and got no response. It could be over, she thought.

But he said, with effort, "As long as I have you…maybe I can figure out what's important."

It wasn't something her ex had ever said. Or anyone else she could remember. This is a breakthrough, she thought.

She did a dope slap, to keep from crying, "Duh, of course, what's going to prevent those particles from the sun from stripping away Earth's atmosphere, too? We have to save our atmosphere. Is there enough oxygen in the spacecraft? We have to dock together." She was babbling.

He said *hmph* softly in her ear. "You're a good listener," he said. "Module coming in to dock. Permission to enter," he said.

SHE REALIZED THAT *hmph* was a small laugh. "It's so polite in space. It's nice to ask permission first. Am I the spaceship?" she said. "Are you going to knock first?"

He let out a groan, having already entered. He managed to say, "What?"

"Never mind," she said, "I'll just keep talking and…\" It seemed right to begin to lose track of what they were saying. "Just keep… keep knocking."

~~

ROBERT SHAPARD has been cocreator and editor with James Thomas of *Sudden* and *Flash Fiction* anthologies for W. W. Norton for many years. He is the author of

Water Issues and Other Safety Concerns. This collection won the W. S. Porter Prize from Regal House Publishing and is due out in Spring 2025. Other stories of his have appeared in *Necessary Fiction, Hoctok, New Flash Fiction Review, Juked, 100 Word Story, New World Writing Quarterly, The Literary Review, Fiction International, The Journal of Compressed Creative Arts, New England Review, Mid-American Review, Kenyon Review, Cimarron Review*, and elsewhere.

19

Muse

EMILY ANDERSON ULA

I have this dream: We're back in the church of Santa Margherita de' Cerchi. You've written a letter to Beatrice Portinari on a receipt for leather shoes—requesting our love last through this life and the next. Me, I don't pray this way. I go down to the river, which morphs into a highway, and stick out my thumb.

In this dream, there's traffic on the Arno. Bumper to bumper. Tourist board conveyances.

Me, I just float on my back. I've always been easy like that. A man on the bridge mistakes me for a vessel and asks if he can come aboard. He looks like you. An idealist. You're all the same, really. Searching for a muse.

"All full," I tell him. This sounds a bit harsh, so I toot-toot an imaginary horn and tip an imaginary hat, compelled to be cordial. A curse.

Up ahead, a woman beneath a parasol points to a rat in the water. "My God, it can swim, Charles!" The gondolier winks at me and shouts, "It's ah-Mickey Mouse!" His standard joke for American tourists. For some reason, my heart swoons with love for him.

I STILL THINK of that day in Florence. An afternoon stop on the rattling train to Lucca. I wanted to see the *David*, but the replica outside the Accademia was just as good, I agreed. I ordered an Aperol spritz at a café near the Duomo. You said my accent was wrong.

I THINK OF Beatrice. How you would call me by her name. Featherbrained, ethereal Beatrice. So sweetly uninhabited, bless her heart. I can still see you at that altar, where she's not even buried. This is where I left you. My soul got hungry and wandered off in search of sustenance. It was like kicking off my shoes.

～～

EMILY ANDERSON ULA is a writer and a speech-language pathologist. She earned her MFA in fiction writing from The University of the South, Sewanee and was the recipient of the School of Letters Rivendell Fellowship Award. Her stories have been published in *The Cincinnati Review*, *The Baltimore Review*, *Pithead Chapel*, *Northwest Review*, *Passages North*, *Flash Fiction Online*, and elsewhere. She can be found on Twitter at @emilyjaneula.

20

Something to See

ALBERTO VOURVOULIAS

* *Suit jacket and pants. White shirt.*
* *Brown knit tie, too narrow, too long.*
* *Pocket square, folded and stapled into shape.*
* *Battered Florsheim wingtips with white athletic socks—a sign of decline.*

This is how my father dressed at proper occasions: dinners out, sales calls, any meeting with money on the line. He married my mother in one. Buried her in another.

The duty nurse hands me his clothes and a battered leather briefcase in an overlarge plastic bag. He hadn't informed me of the procedure. The neighbor he'd enlisted to pick him up afterward called. "Your father is dead," she said. "I can't stay. I have to get home to make dinner for my family."

Father's body is cold by the time I arrive at the hospital. His skin glistens like bee's wax, sluggish to the touch, soft and inert. I find my way to the address listed on his driver's license. The efficiency is hard-scrubbed and pin-neat. It smells of lemons. The bed's made with a military tuck. There's a card in a blank envelope on the bare kitchen table. "I Love You" is the preprinted message. No name. No signature. No instructions.

- *Wash the hospital stink out of the clothes.*
- *Lay them flat on the mattress in the shape of a man.*

I'd seen him a handful of times in 15 years. I sleep on the couch, unwilling to rumple the last careful thing he'd done. In the morning, I force the briefcase with a hammer, after failing to guess the combination. The case was an extension of his body, a portable organ where he secreted treasures.

- *Three legal pads, yellow lined paper, unmarked.*
- *One silver Cross pen, blue ink.*
- *Two packs of Post-its, one pink, one yellow.*

On the rare occasion that he sent me a letter, it consisted of a note affixed to an article torn from a newspaper: "Thought you might be interested." Or a bill that had lost its way: "This came for you. Opened by mistake."

- *Half a dozen sales brochures for hearing aids and vitamin supplements—products he sold but refused to use.*
- *Mother's wedding band zippered into a mesh side compartment. Father's, taken from his swollen finger on the operating table, glimmers in my pocket.*
- *Keys to the old house, long sold.*
- *A religious medal, St. Christopher. Must have been a gift from her.*

She was the church regular; he, the pagan who believed in a god of motion. At her funeral, Father consoled me by saying, "She gets to rest. We keep going."

I didn't go far. Back to school, then to a job I would quit and a wife who would leave me. Every Sunday, I joined him for early dinner. We sat across from each other, trusting to silence more than words. We each bussed our own plates and watched the Phillies or the Eagles on the tube. Then, every two or four. Then, not at all.

Father pushed into new sales schemes and territories, each more far-fetched and far-flung. I came to think that it had been us who had died.

- *Certificate of Birth, Honey Brook, PA, 77 years ago.*
- *Honorable discharge—which entitles Father to a flag every Memorial Day. I never asked if he had killed someone for the privilege.*
- *Last will and testament, duly signed and witnessed, leaving all to me.*

The last time I saw you alive, Father, you rang my apartment buzzer without warning in the middle of a hurricane. We chased Ida's track through Pennsylvania and New Jersey. We drove through wind and rain so thick it lashed like waves. We skirted flooded fields and rolled by homes torn open by fallen branches. We passed great oaks toppled in the mud and vast whirls of uprooted stalks.

When I finally got up the courage to ask, you said, "I just thought that it was something you ought to see."

ALBERTO VOURVOULIAS was born in Mexico and grew up in Guatemala. He was brought to the US at 16. He's worked as a journalist in both Spanish and English-language media and has taught in the master's program in bilingual journalism at CUNY. He's also taught courses in politics at Yale University and in the New Jersey prison system.